HIGH-FLYING
HELICOPTERS

For Louie Ronald Ellwood Cope—T.M.
For Wilf—A.P.

KINGFISHER
LONDON & NEW YORK

Text copyright © Tony Mitton 2016
Illustrations copyright © Ant Parker 2016
Designed by Anthony Hannant (LittleRedAnt) 2016
Published in the United States by Kingfisher,
175 Fifth Ave., New York, NY 10010
Kingfisher is an imprint of Macmillan Children's Books, London.
All rights reserved.
Distributed in the U.S. and Canada by Macmillan, 175 Fifth Ave., New York, NY 10010

Library of Congress Cataloging-in-Publication data have been applied for.

ISBN 978-0-7534-7290-3 (HB)
ISBN 978-0-7534-7291-0 (PB)

Kingfisher books are available for special promotions and premiums. For details contact:
Special Markets Department, Macmillan, 175 Fifth Ave., New York, NY 10010.

For more information, please visit
www.kingfisherbooks.com

Printed in China
9 8 7 6 5 4 3 2 1
1TR/0516/HH/UG/128MA

HIGH-FLYING HELICOPTERS

Tony Mitton and
Ant Parker

KINGFISHER
NEW YORK

Helicopters hovering, hanging in the sky—

clattering and racketing,
they hover low and high.

A helicopter's rotor blades
create the lift and rise.

They press upon the air to send it
riding through the skies.

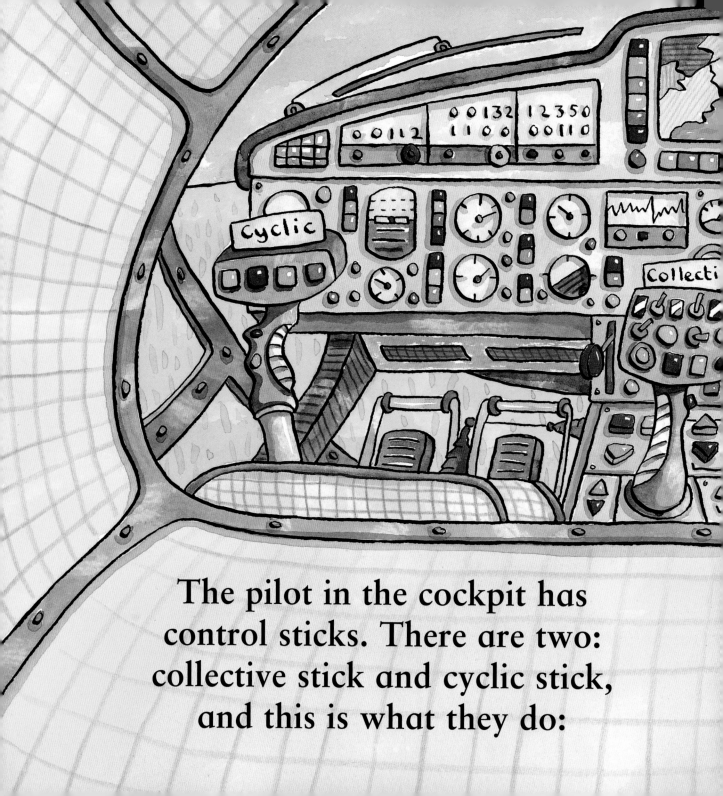

The pilot in the cockpit has
control sticks. There are two:
collective stick and cyclic stick,
and this is what they do:

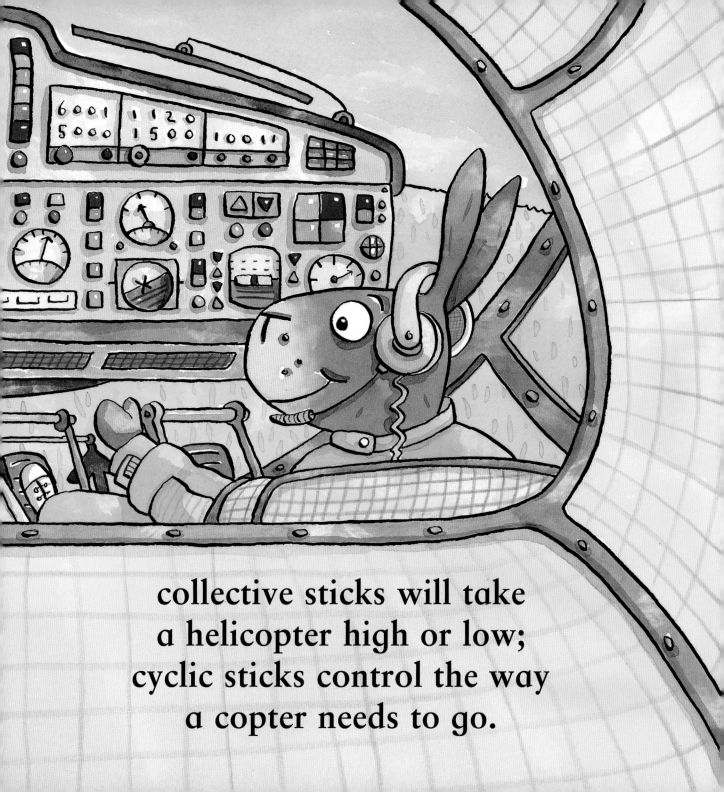

collective sticks will take
a helicopter high or low;
cyclic sticks control the way
a copter needs to go.

For copters can go forward,
backward, sideways, up, or down,

which means they're great for
tricky things in country or in town.

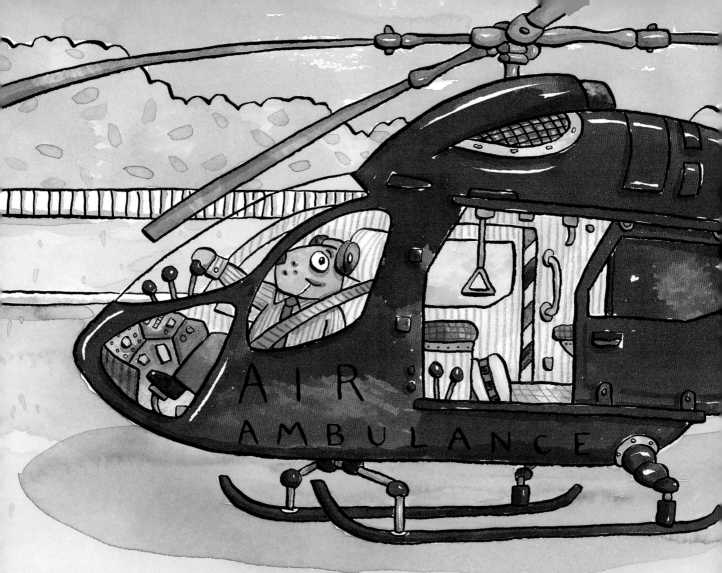

This copter is an ambulance.
When patients need quick care,
if streets are slow a copter
can deliver them by air.

This copter uses radar
to scan the stormy seas.

It winches folks to safety when they've
signaled, "Help us, please!"

This mountain rescue copter goes
to places high and snowy.

It rescues people stranded where the
weather's chill and blowy.

And here's a helicopter scooping water from a lake.

You need a lot of water with a
forest fire to break.

Police use helicopters
to observe things on the ground.
Their cameras are good for trailing
cars and folks around.

They sometimes use a searchlight
to show things on the go,
and radio their ground crew
who are busy down below.

This shuttle helicopter is
a taxi in the sky.

It's come to take us on a trip.
It's time to say good-bye.

Helicopter parts

tail rotor
this helps the helicopter change direction—some helicopters have a fan inside the tail

rotor blade
the rotor has two, three, or four of these—they spin round like fan blades

cockpit
this is where the pilot sits to control the helicopter

tail boom
this helps balance the helicopter when it flies—and keeps the two rotors well apart

skids
the helicopter rests on these when it lands, but some helicopters have wheels

cabin
this is where the passengers or goods travel

Collect all the **AMAZING MACHINES** books by Tony Mitton and Ant Parker!

 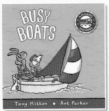    

HC ISBN 978-0-7534-5403-9 TP ISBN 978-0-7534-5916-4 HC ISBN 978-0-7534-5802-0 TP ISBN 978-0-7534-5304-9 TP ISBN 978-0-7534-5307-0 HC ISBN 978-0-7534-7290-3
TP ISBN 978-0-7534-5915-7   TP ISBN 978-0-7534-7207-1   TP ISBN 978-0-7534-7291-0

     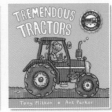

HC ISBN 978-0-7534-7292-7 TP ISBN 978-0-7534-5305-6 TP ISBN 978-0-7534-7208-8 TP ISBN 978-0-7534-5306-3 TP ISBN 978-0-7534-5917-1 TP ISBN 978-0-7534-5918-8
TP ISBN 978-0-7534-7293-4

Younger children will love these **AMAZING MACHINES** board books:

    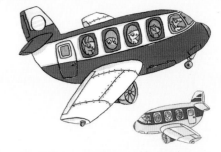

ISBN 978-0-7534-7233-0 ISBN 978-0-7534-7231-6 ISBN 978-0-7534-7234-7 ISBN 978-0-7534-7232-3

Get busy with the **AMAZING MACHINES** activity books—with a model to make and stickers!

   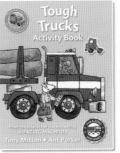 

ISBN 978-0-7534-7255-2 ISBN 978-0-7534-7256-9 ISBN 978-0-7534-7257-6 ISBN 978-0-7534-7254-5